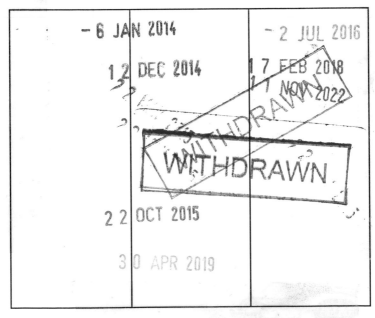

For Daniel Barrie ~ D R

For Liz and Stephen – Our Friends in

the North ~ A M

STRIPES PUBLISHING
An imprint of Little Tiger Press
1 The Coda Centre, 189 Munster Road,
London SW6 6AW

A paperback original
First published in Great Britain in 2011

Characters created by David Roberts
Text copyright © Alan MacDonald, 2011
Illustrations copyright © David Roberts, 2011

ISBN: 978-1-84715-167-4

Printed and bound in the UK.

10 9 8 7 6 5 4 3

Dirty Bertie

OUCH!

DAVID ROBERTS WRITTEN BY ALAN MACDONALD

stripes

Collect all the
Dirty Bertie books!

Worms!
Fleas!
Pants!
Burp!
Yuck!
Crackers!
Bogeys!
Mud!
Germs!
Loo!
Fetch!
Fangs!
Kiss!
Snow!
Pong!
Pirate!
Scream!
Toothy!
My Joke Book
My Book of Stuff

Contents

1   Ouch!   7

2   Bottom!   37

3   Brainiac!   67

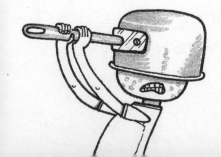

CHAPTER 1

"Go on," said Darren. "I dare you. Before he comes back."

Bertie looked at the hammer.
It belonged to Mr Grouch, the demon caretaker. Bertie and Darren were helping him with the scenery for the school play. So far they had done nothing but stand around listening to the caretaker grumble.

But Mr Grouch wasn't around right now. He'd gone off to fetch more nails, leaving his hammer lying on the stage.

"Why don't you do it?" asked Bertie.

"I dared you first," said Darren.

"I dare you back," said Bertie.

"I double dare you no returns," said Darren.

Bertie looked around. He never refused a dare, not even the time Darren dared him to lock Mr Weakly in the store cupboard. And this was just one little tap with a hammer. What harm could it do? A nail was sticking up practically begging to be hit. Bertie picked up the hammer and took a swing.

"Watch what you're doing!" cried Darren, ducking out of the way.

"Well, stand back then," said Bertie.
"I need room."

He glanced round, checking that no
one was about. All clear.

DINK! He tapped the nail on the head.

Darren rolled his eyes. "Not like that!
Give it a proper whack."

Bertie held the nail between his finger and thumb. He swung the hammer back and brought it down.

THUNK!

"YOWWWWW!" he wailed, dropping the hammer. "What did you do?" said Darren.

"I HIT MY THUMB! ARGH! OWW!" Bertie hopped around like a frog on a dance floor.

"SHHH!" hissed Darren. "Someone will hear you!"

Bertie was in too much pain to care. "OWW! OWW! OWW!" he howled.

Footsteps came thudding down the corridor. Mr Grouch burst into the hall, followed by Miss Boot.

"WHAT IS GOING ON?" yelled Miss Boot.

"Nothing, Miss," said Darren.

"ARGH! OHHHH!" cried Bertie, doubled over in pain.

Mr Grouch spotted the hammer on the floor.

"Have you been playing with this?" he growled, picking it up.

Darren shook his head. "No," he said. "I haven't!"

Miss Boot turned on Bertie. "Did you touch this hammer?"

"I was only trying to help!" moaned Bertie.

"I knew it!" cried Mr Grouch. "I turn my back for two seconds and this is what happens. That boy is a menace. He should be expelled!"

"Yes, thank you, Mr Grouch," said Miss Boot. "I will deal with this."

"OWW! OWW!" wailed Bertie. "I think it's broken!"

"Don't make such a fuss!" snapped Miss Boot. "Let me see."

Bertie let go of his thumb and held it out for inspection. Yikes! It had turned purple and swollen up like a balloon! "I don't feel very well," he said, going pale.

Miss Boot took charge. "Darren, take him to Miss Skinner's office," she ordered. "And Bertie, don't think you've heard the last of this, I shall be speaking to your parents."

♭   ♪   ♩

Bertie sat outside Miss Skinner's office nursing his injured thumb. It was wrapped in a wet paper towel. He couldn't believe the way everyone was remaining so calm. Why hadn't they called an ambulance? For all they knew he could be dying!

The door flew open and his mum hurried in.

"Bertie, are you all right?" she cried.

Bertie shook his head weakly and held up his hand.

"I think it's broken!" he moaned.

"Your hand?"

"My thumb."

"Well, what happened?"

"It wasn't my fault," said Bertie. "I was trying to help. The hammer slipped."

"Hammer!" shrieked Mum. "What on earth were you doing with a hammer?"

"Hammering," replied Bertie.

"Well next time, *don't*. Hammers are dangerous," said Mum. "Let me see."

Bertie gingerly unwrapped the soggy paper towel. His thumb was still swollen.

Mum stared. "Is that it?" she said. "I thought it was serious!"

"It hurts!" said Bertie. "It's probably broken!"

"So you keep saying," sighed Mum. "Well, we'd better get it checked out. Let's get you to hospital."

CHAPTER 2

Later that afternoon, Bertie sat in the hospital waiting room. It was packed with people. Bertie stared at a small girl with her foot in plaster. Beside her was a man in a neck collar and a boy with a saucepan jammed on his head. You got all kinds of people in hospitals. Bertie checked his thumb again to see if it had got any bigger. It hadn't.

He looked at the clock. They had been waiting for hours and he hadn't eaten since lunch. His stomach gurgled. If they waited much longer he might pass out with hunger. Tempting smells drifted across from the snack bar.

"Mum, can I get some crisps?" asked Bertie.

"No," said Mum. "I thought you were in agony."

"I AM," said Bertie. "But crisps might take my mind off it."

Mum gave him a weary look. "You're not having crisps now," she said.

Bertie sighed. "How about a doughnut, then?"

"NO, BERTIE!" snapped Mum. "Just sit quietly and wait for the doctor."

Bertie slumped in his seat. Talking about food only made him hungrier. Maybe he could just investigate what the snack bar had to offer? He got up.

"Where are you going?" asked Mum, lowering her magazine.

"Nowhere! Just to have a look," pleaded Bertie.

"Well, stay where I can keep an eye on you," said Mum.

There was a queue of people at the counter. Bertie hung around for a while, hoping someone might take pity on a starving boy. No one did. On a nearby table he noticed a bowl containing small packets of mayonnaise, tomato ketchup and mustard. Bertie slipped a couple of them into his pocket as emergency supplies for later. He looked up and

found a boy with his arm in a sling
watching him.

"What happened to you?" asked
Bertie.

The boy shrugged. "Hit a lamp post."

"With your arm?" said Bertie.

"No, on my bike," said the boy.

"I hit my thumb with a hammer," said
Bertie, proudly. He unwound the paper
towel to show off his swollen thumb.

The boy shrugged. "Huh! That's nothing," he scoffed. "I'm always in hospital. This is the second time I broke my arm. Broke my collar bone too."

"Wow!" said Bertie, impressed. The only thing he'd ever broken was the upstairs toilet.

The boy lowered his voice. "They don't let you stay unless it's serious," he said.

"Stay where?" said Bertie.

"On the children's ward." The boy gave him a pitying look. "Haven't you ever been in hospital?"

Bertie shook his head.

"You don't know what you're missing!" said the boy. "You don't have to do nothing – just lie in bed all day, watching TV. No going to school – nothing."

Bertie gawped at the boy. Staying in

hospital sounded like paradise! Much
better than listening to Miss Boot
droning on for hours. Maybe the hospital
would keep him in for a few days, or
even a week? He noticed his mum
beckoning him to sit down.

"Better go," he said.

The boy nodded. "Okay. Maybe catch
you on the children's ward later?"

"I'll be there," said Bertie.

He went back to his seat.

"Who was that?" asked Mum.

"Don't know," replied Bertie. "We just
got talking. Mum, how long do you think
I'll have to stay in hospital?"

Mum laughed. "Bertie, you've only
bruised your thumb!"

"It might be broken," Bertie reminded
her.

Mum shook her head. "If it was, you'd be in agony."

"I *am* in agony!" said Bertie. "I'm just not making a fuss!"

"You fooled me," said Mum. "In any case, they'll probably just give you a plaster and send you home."

Bertie stared. Send him home with a plaster? They couldn't do that! What about missing school?

CHAPTER 3

"BERTIE BURNS?" called a loud voice.
Bertie looked up. A red-haired nurse
with a clipboard was looking round the
waiting room. Her badge said "Nurse
Nettles".

"Over here!" said Mum, standing up.

"Follow me, would you please?" said
the nurse.

Bertie and Mum followed her down the corridor and into a cubicle with a bed, a table and a couple of plastic chairs. The nurse drew the curtain across and looked briskly at Bertie.

"Well, young man, what have you been up to?" she said.

"Nothing," frowned Bertie. "I hurt my thumb."

"He hit it with a hammer," explained Mum.

"Not on purpose," said Bertie. The way everyone talked you'd think he had.

Nurse Nettles wrote something on a form. "Let's have a look at it then, shall we?" she said.

Bertie winced as Nurse Nettles unwound the paper towel. The thumb was still purple, though not quite as swollen as Bertie remembered.

"Mmm, yes, I see," said Nurse Nettles.
"Try and move it for me."

Bertie waggled his thumb gingerly.

"OUCH!" he yelled.

"Now bend it back."

Bertie bent it back.

"ARGHH!"

"Well?" asked Mum. "Is it serious?"

Nurse Nettles smiled. "I don't think so.
Badly bruised, that's all."

"BRUISED?" cried Bertie. "Not broken?"

"Not broken," said Nurse Nettles. "But we'll get Dr Dose to examine you."

This was more like it.

"Does that mean I have to stay in hospital?" asked Bertie.

Nurse Nettles laughed. "No, don't worry, you'll be going home in no time."

She went off to find the doctor.

Bertie slumped back on the bed. Bruised? Was that all? It was so unfair! After all the pain he'd been through! Had Nurse Nettles actually looked at his thumb properly? It was purple! Did they really expect him to go to school with a purple thumb? What he needed was a proper rest – rest and unlimited television.

"You see?" said Mum. "I told you it was nothing to worry about."

Bertie scowled. If only his thumb was hanging off, spurting fountains of blood everywhere. If only it had gone bad and was dripping with yellow pus. Wait a moment… Bertie felt in his pocket. He still had the little packets he'd got from the snack bar. Mustard was yellow. All he needed was a minute to himself, before the doctor came.

He jumped to his feet.
"I need the toilet!" he said.

"What? Now?" said Mum. "Can't you wait?"

"No!" said Bertie. "Won't be a minute."
He dashed off.

CHAPTER 4

By the time Bertie got back, Dr Dose
had arrived and was talking to his mum
and Nurse Nettles.

"Right then," said Dr Dose, rubbing his
hands. "Let's have a look at this thumb,
shall we?"

Bertie nodded weakly and held it up
for him to see.

Dirty Bertie

"Good heavens!" said Nurse Nettles.

Bertie's thumb had turned a funny colour. Globs of yellow oozed and dripped on to the floor.

"What happened?" cried Mum.

"I don't know!" groaned Bertie. "I think it's infected!"

Dr Dose pushed his glasses up his nose. "It does look odd. Let me see."

He peered closely at the thumb. "Cotton wool, please, nurse," he said.

He dabbed at the messy thumb and sniffed the cotton wool.

"Ah," he said. "Just as I thought. Mustarditis."

Nurse Nettles giggled.

Bertie looked up at them. "Is that bad?"

"Very bad," said Doctor Dose.

"Mustarditis?" repeated Mum.

Dr Dose gave her a wink. "Perhaps you could wait outside while I talk to Bertie."

"Yes, I think *someone* should," said Mum.

Bertie sat on the bed. His brilliant trick had fooled everyone. *Children's ward, here I come!* he thought. *A whole week off school!*

"Will I have to stay in hospital?" he asked, feebly.

"For a while," said Dr Dose. "After the operation."

Bertie gasped. Operation? No one had said anything about an operation!

"W-what?" he mumbled.

"Well, your thumb's turned yellow," said Dr Dose. "Very bad, mustarditis. The only thing is to operate right away. Wouldn't you agree, Nurse Nettles?"

Nurse Nettles nodded, trying not to laugh.

Bertie stared at them. All he wanted was a few days off school – not this! He imagined the operating theatre. There would be an injection – with a long needle. Doctors in masks. What if they decided his thumb couldn't be saved? What if they chopped it off? He needed his thumb to beat Darren at Mega Monster Racing!

Dr Dose put something on. It was a green mask.

"Right," he said brightly. "Shall we get started?"

"NOOO!" cried Bertie, leaping off the bed.

He rushed through the curtains, hurrying past his mum, who was waiting outside.

"HELP! SAVE ME!" he gasped. "Don't let them get me!"

"I thought your thumb was agony," said Mum.

"No!" said Bertie. "Look, it's better!" He licked his thumb. "It was only mustard."

Dr Dose and Nurse Nettles peered through the curtains. They were laughing and wiping their eyes. Bertie gaped. The truth dawned on him. There was no operation – it was all a joke.

"So," said Mum. "Mustard, eh?"

"Um, yes," said Bertie. "I must have somehow got a bit on my thumb."

"Really? I wonder how that could have happened," said Mum dryly.

"Never mind," said Nurse Nettles brightly. "Let's find you a plaster, shall we?"

Dirty Bertie

Bertie went back to sit on the bed. A plaster – after all he'd been through! He'd told Darren his thumb was broken and by now the story would be all round school. No one was going to be very impressed if he came back wearing a stupid little plaster.

Nurse Nettles looked in a drawer. She held out a plaster the size of a postage stamp. Bertie looked at her.

"Actually," he said, "you don't have something a bit bigger, do you?"

BOTTOM!

CHAPTER 1

"LAST ONE CHANGED IS A
STINKER!" shouted Darren.

Bertie banged into the cubicle and
dumped his bag on the seat. It was Friday
– swimming day. He stripped off his
clothes, dropping them in a messy heap.
Then he picked up his bag and emptied
it out. Goggles, towel, shower gel…

Wait a minute, where were his swimming trunks? His heart missed a beat. He picked up his towel and shook it out. Nothing! He searched the bottom of his bag. Empty! Surely he hadn't ... he couldn't have left his swimming trunks at home? Miss Boot would go up the wall!

He wrapped a towel round his waist and climbed on to the seat.

"Psssst! Eugene!" he hissed, peering into the next cubicle.

"What?" Eugene blinked at him through his goggles.

"I forgot my trunks!" said Bertie.

"You're joking!" said Eugene.

Darren's head popped up from the next cubicle along. "What's going on?"

"Bertie's forgotten his trunks," explained Eugene.

"You haven't!"

"I HAVE!" groaned Bertie. "You've got to help! Miss Boot will kill me!"

His friends nodded grimly. A few weeks ago Trevor had forgotten his towel. Miss Boot had made him do twenty laps of the changing room to dry off.

"What am I going to do?" moaned Bertie.

Darren shrugged. "You'll just have to wear your pants."

Bertie gave him a look. "I can't swim in my pants!" he said. His pants had holes in them and, besides, they looked like … well, like pants. He turned to Eugene.

"Didn't you bring a spare pair?"

"Why would I do that?" asked Eugene.

"So I can borrow them, of course!"

Eugene shook his head.

"Darren, what about you?" pleaded Bertie.

"Sorry, can't help," said Darren.

Bertie gave a heavy sigh. He was sunk.

There was a loud bang on the changing-room door.

"ONE MINUTE! GET A MOVE ON!" bellowed Miss Boot.

"Sorry, Bertie, we better go," said Eugene. "You know how mad she gets if you're late."

Dirty Bertie

"Yeah," said Darren. "Good luck!"

The two of them hurried out, leaving Bertie alone. He slumped on the seat in despair. Suddenly, an ugly face appeared in the gap under the door. It was Know-All Nick, the last person on earth he wanted to see.

"Oh dear, Bertie, forgotten your swimming trunks?" he jeered. "Wait till Miss Boot finds out!" He disappeared, sniggering to himself.

Bertie sank back against the wall. Maybe if he just stayed here, he wouldn't be missed and the swimming lesson would go ahead without him. Afterwards he could wet his hair under the tap and slip on to the coach.

WHAM! The changing-room door flew open. Footsteps thudded down the corridor.

"BERTIE! WHERE ARE YOU?" boomed Miss Boot. "Come out of there!"

"I can't!" moaned Bertie. "I haven't got any trunks!"

Miss Boot raised her eyes to heaven. Why did it always have to be Bertie?

"Open this door!" she ordered.

Bertie slid back the lock and peeped out, holding the towel round his waist.

"Couldn't I just sit and watch?" he pleaded.

"Certainly not!" snapped Miss Boot. "You'll just have to borrow some trunks."

"I've tried!" said Bertie. "No one's got
any."

"Then go to Reception and ask them
to lend you a pair," said Miss Boot. "And
get a move on. Everyone's waiting!"

Bertie nodded and shuffled past Miss
Boot. As he reached the door, he trod
on his towel.

"Bertie!" Miss Boot groaned and
covered her eyes.

CHAPTER 2

Bertie stood in Reception. The woman behind the desk was talking on the phone.

"Yes? Can I help you?" she said, putting it down at last.

"Um ... yes," said Bertie, "I don't have any swimming trunks."

"Oh dear!" said the woman. "Didn't you bring them?"

45

"I forgot," said Bertie. "They're probably at home – in my pants drawer."

"Well, you're not allowed in the pool without a costume, it's against the rules," said the woman.

"I know," said Bertie. "But Miss Boot said you might have some swimming trunks I could borrow."

"I see," sighed the woman. She looked at her coffee, which was getting cold. "Wait there," she said. "I'll see what I can do."

Bertie waited. It was embarrassing standing in the middle of Reception, wearing only a towel. A small girl over by the drinks machine was staring at him. Finally, the woman came back carrying a large green box, marked "Lost Property". She put it down on the floor.

Dirty Bertie

"Here we are," she said. "There's not much, but take your pick."

Bertie peered inside. The box contained a pair of orange water wings, a swimming cap, a spotty bikini and a single pair of swimming trunks. Bertie fished them out. They were silver Speedos, hardly bigger than a paper tissue.

"Is this all there is?" he gasped.

The woman sniffed. "Looks like it."

"But haven't you got anything else? Like normal swimming shorts?"

The woman glared. "We're not a shop!" she snapped. "Do you want them or not?"

Bertie nodded miserably. He had no choice. He shuffled back to the changing room, holding the trunks as if they were riddled with fleas. Wait till his friends saw him! He was going to be the laughing stock of the whole class.

He locked himself inside the cubicle and pulled on the silver trunks. They were so old that the elastic had gone, and no matter how tightly he tied them, they wouldn't stay up! He looked down in horror. There was no way he could wear these.

Someone thumped on the door.
"BERTIE! HURRY UP!" thundered Miss
Boot. "WE'RE WAITING FOR YOU!"

Bertie groaned. He opened the
cubicle door and slunk out.

Miss Boot stared. "What on earth are
those?" she said.

"Swimming trunks," wailed Bertie. "It's
all they had!"

"Very well, they'll have to do," said Miss Boot. "Pull them up and let's go."

The class were sitting by the side of the pool, with their feet in the water. Miss Crawl leaned against the rail, impatient to get started. She was a tall, thin woman who had once been Junior Backstroke Champion.

Everyone looked round as Bertie appeared. He ducked behind Miss Boot, but it was too late. Know-All Nick had seen him.

"HA HA! LOOK AT BERTIE!" he hooted.

"Nice trunks, Bertie!" giggled Donna.

"Are they your grandad's?" screeched Trevor.

Bertie glared at them and plodded over to join the end of the line.

Dirty Bertie

"Oh, Bertie," sang Nick. "We can see your bottom!"

Bertie went bright red and hitched up the saggy Speedos. This was terrible! How was he going to get through an entire swimming lesson without dying of embarrassment?

CHAPTER 3

Bertie clung to the side of the pool, shivering with cold. The lesson had only been going half an hour, but it felt like a lifetime. He had hardly dared leave the side for fear of losing his trunks.

Know-All Nick zoomed past, splashing him in the face.

"BERTIE!" bellowed a voice.

Uh oh, Miss Boot had spotted him.

"What are you doing?" she called.
"Miss Crawl, why isn't Bertie joining in?"

"Good question," said Miss Crawl.
"Bertie, what do you think you're doing?"

"Nothing," said Bertie.

"Well, get away from the side. I said four lengths' breaststroke!"

"I can't!" wailed Bertie.

"Why not?"

"My trunks keep falling down!"

"No feeble excuses!" snapped Miss Crawl. "Get swimming!"

Bertie groaned. He pushed off and swam after the rest of the class. ARGHH! The saggy Speedos were falling down again! He could feel them slipping towards his knees. He tried swimming with one hand while holding on to the stupid trunks with the other. It was hard work. He kept sinking and glugging great gulps of water.

"Come on, Bertie, keep up!" shouted Darren, speeding past.

At last he made it to the far end and hung on to the rail, gasping for breath. Know-All Nick climbed out by the steps.

He hurried over to Miss Crawl,
dripping wet.

"Miss! OOOH! OOH! I need the
toilet!" he whimpered.

Miss Crawl scowled. "Can't you hang
on?"

"No! I've got to goooo!" cried Nick,
jiggling from foot to foot.

"Oh, very well!" sighed Miss Crawl. "Hurry up!"

Bertie watched Nick patter off towards the changing room. Suddenly, he was struck by an idea. It was so simple it was genius. But he'd have to move fast or it would be too late. Bertie swam to the steps and climbed out.

"What now?" said Miss Crawl.

"Miss! I need the toilet, Miss!" pleaded Bertie.

"Not you as well? You'll just have to wait till the lesson is over."

"But I can't!" said Bertie, dancing up and down. "I have to go! NOW!"

Miss Crawl sighed heavily. "Go on then. Make it quick!"

Dirty Bertie

Bertie pushed open the changing-room door. There was no one about. He stole over to the boys' toilets. He could hear Know-All Nick humming to himself in one of the cubicles. Bertie tiptoed over. He got down on his hands and knees to peer under the door. There were Nick's two white feet dangling in mid-air, with his red swimming trunks round his ankles.

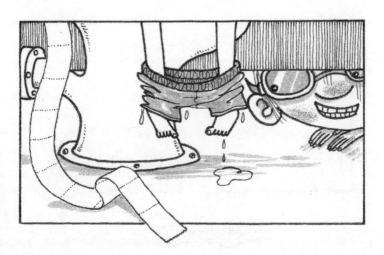

"Hmm hmm hmm!" Nick hummed to himself.

Slowly, silently, Bertie reached his hand under the door.

SNATCH!

He grabbed the red swimming trunks and yanked them off.

"ARGHHH!" cried Nick, overbalancing and falling off the toilet.

"HEY! GIVE THEM BACK!" he howled. "THEY'RE MINE!"

"Sorry, Nickerless!" replied Bertie. "I need them."

Nick banged on the door. "I'll tell!" he yelled. "You give them back, Bertie, or I'll tell!"

There was no reply.

Cautiously, Know-All Nick unlocked the door and came out. Bertie had vanished. All that remained was a soggy pair of Speedos lying on the floor.

CHAPTER 4

Back in the pool, Bertie joined the rest of the class.

PEEP! Miss Crawl blew her whistle. "Everyone out! Line up by the side!"

Eugene climbed out after Bertie. "Where did you get those trunks?" he asked, in surprise. "I thought yours were teeny-weeny."

Bertie grinned. "I'll tell you later."

"Right," said Miss Crawl. "I want you all to try the standing dive we did last week."

"Just a minute!" Miss Boot had been counting heads. "We're missing someone," she said. "Where is Nicholas?"

Miss Crawl frowned. "He went to the toilet, but that was ages ago."

Miss Boot marched over to the boys' changing room. She pounded on the door.

THUMP! THUMP!

"Nicholas? Are you in there?"

No answer.

"NICHOLAS! Come out!"

"I CAN'T!" wailed a voice.

"Nonsense! What's the matter with you?" barked Miss Boot.

"I haven't got any trunks!"

"Don't be ridiculous, you were

wearing them earlier. Come out this instant!"

"Please don't make me!" snivelled Nick.

But Miss Boot was not a patient woman. "If you're not out in ten seconds I shall come in and drag you out," she warned.

The door opened slowly and Know-All Nick shuffled out. He was covering

himself with a small yellow towel.

"Line up then!" ordered Miss Boot.

"But Miss, Bertie's—"

"Line up, I said! You're keeping everyone waiting!"

Know-All Nick gulped. He drooped over to join the line and put down his towel. He was wearing the saggy silver Speedos.

"HA HA!" hooted Bertie.

"Hee hee! Nice trunks, Nick!" giggled Darren.

"QUIET!" bawled Miss Crawl. "On my whistle, you will all dive in. Arms out, knees bent, heads down."

PEEP!

SPLASH! SPLOOSH! The class flopped into the pool one by one. Bertie bobbed to the surface and wiped his eyes. Something was floating on top of the water. A pair of silver swimming trunks. Bertie fished them out and waved them in the air.

"OH, NICKERLESS!" he cried. "DID YOU LOSE SOMETHING?"

Dirty Bertie

BRAINIAC!

SWOTTER

18

PUDSLEY

01

CHAPTER 1

It was Tuesday morning. Miss Boot put away the register and took out a letter.

"I have some good news for you," she said. "In two weeks' time it's the Junior Quiz Challenge and we will be entering a team."

The class turned pale. Bertie groaned. Of all the horrible tortures teachers

had invented, the worst was the Junior
Quiz Challenge. Four children forced on
to a stage and made to answer endless
impossible questions: What is the capital
of Belgium? How many minutes in a
fortnight? Can you spell "ignoramus"?

Every year Pudsley Junior entered a
quiz team and every year they came
bottom. Last time they'd scored a grand
total of two and a half points – a record
low in the history of the competition.
A picture of the team had appeared in
the *Pudsley Post* under the headline:
"QUIZ FLOPS COME BOTTOM OF
THE CLASS!"
Miss Boot had been furious. Miss Skinner
said they'd brought shame on the
whole school.

Bertie slid down in his chair. There was

no way he wanted to be on the team.
He'd rather dance down the high street
dressed as a fairy. But wait a second, why
did he need to worry? Miss Boot never
picked him for anything.

"Hands up," said Miss Boot, "who'd like
to be on the quiz team?"

Only one hand went up. It belonged
to Know-All Nick. *Trust smarty-pants Nick
to volunteer*, thought Bertie.

"Nicholas!" beamed Miss Boot.
"Marvellous! I knew you
would set an example."

Nick's head swelled
even larger than usual.

"Who else? What about you, Donna?"
asked Miss Boot.

"Umm…" said Donna.

"Excellent!" said Miss Boot. "And
Eugene, I'm sure you'd be good!"

"Er … ah … mmm," mumbled Eugene.

"Splendid! That's three then," said Miss
Boot. "So we just need one more to
complete the team." Her gaze swept
over the rows of faces. The class shrank
back, desperate to avoid her eye. Darren
raised his hand.

"What about Bertie, Miss?" he asked.

Bertie spun round. "Me? Are you
mad?" He glared at Darren. Then he
remembered. Yesterday he had put
superglue on Darren's chair and Darren
had vowed to get his revenge.

Miss Boot frowned. "I don't think so,"

she said. "We need bright, clever children and Bertie is … well, his talents lie in other areas." This was true, thought Bertie. He was the class burping champion and he did a brilliant impression of Miss Boot.

"But, Miss, Bertie is brilliant at quizzes," claimed Darren, grinning at Bertie.

"NO I'M NOT!" cried Bertie.

"You are!" lied Darren. "You've always got your head in a quiz book."

"Thank you, Darren, I'll bear that in mind," said Miss Boot. She turned back to the class. "One more volunteer," she said. "Who'd like to represent our school? Royston?"

Royston shook his head.

"Nisha?"

Nisha hid behind Donna.

"Kylie?"

Kylie looked as if she might be sick.

Miss Boot sighed heavily. "Very well then, Bertie, you're on the team."

"But, Miss…!" moaned Bertie.

"No need to thank me," said Miss Boot. "Just remember, I am giving you a chance, Bertie. Last year's team did not make their school proud. But this year will be different, because you will be prepared. And when the time comes, I expect you to win – is that clear?"

The quiz team nodded their heads gloomily. Bertie glared at Darren. This was so unfair!

CHAPTER 2

DRRRRRING! The bell went for lunchtime. Bertie headed for the door.

"Bertie!" called Know-All Nick. "Quiz team meeting!"

Bertie rolled his eyes and flopped into a chair beside Eugene. Who wanted to be stuck inside listening to Nick, when you could be outside playing?

"Now," said Nick, "Miss Boot told me to choose a team captain. I think we all know who it should be."

"Who?" said Donna.

"Well, me, obviously," said Nick.

"Why you?"

"Because I'm the cleverest," boasted Nick.

"The ugliest, you mean," muttered Bertie.

Nick ignored him. "Practice sessions will be *every* lunchtime, starting today."

"Every lunchtime?" groaned Eugene. "How can we practise for a quiz?"

"By answering test questions, of course," said Nick. "Miss Boot lent me this." He reached into his bag and brought out *The Bumper Book of Quiz Fun.*

"Right, I'll be quiz master," he said.

"And who's testing you?" asked Donna.

"No one, because I'm captain and I've got the book," said Nick. "Anyway, I don't need the practice. Bertie, you can go first because you're the most stupid. Eugene, you time him. You've got one minute."

Eugene set the timer on his watch.

"Donna, you keep the score. Ready?" said Nick, settling on a page in the book. "Go…! Hades was the god of what?"

"Never heard of him," said Bertie.

"He's a Greek god, stupid, like Zeus and Mars."

"Isn't that a chocolate bar?" said Bertie.

"What?"

"Mars."

"Yes! No! I'm asking the questions!" snapped Nick, getting muddled.

"Well, what's the good of asking me stuff I don't know?" grumbled Bertie. "Why don't you try asking me something I do know?"

Nick sighed. "Next question…"

"Time's up!" shouted Eugene.

"And in that round, Bertie, you answered no questions and scored no points!" said Donna.

Bertie took a bow. Eugene clapped.

"Yes, very funny," glowered Nick. "A fat lot of use you're going to be."

After school, Bertie dropped in to see his gran. He told her all about the Junior Quiz Challenge and Miss Boot picking him for the team.

"That's wonderful, Bertie!" said Gran.

"No, it's terrible," said Bertie. "I'm rubbish at quizzes and Miss Boot expects us to win."

"Well, maybe you will," said Gran.

"We won't!" Bertie moaned. "We come last every year!"

Gran sighed. "Tell you what," she said, "why don't we call in at the library and find some books to help you."

Bertie couldn't see how books were going to help, but he didn't have any better ideas.

Dirty Bertie

At the library Gran took him upstairs to the Children's Section.

"So what kind of things do you like?" she asked.

Bertie shrugged. "Loads of things," he said. "Worms, slugs, maggots, stink-bombs…"

"Hmm," said Gran. "Somehow I doubt stink-bombs are going to help."

Dirty Bertie

Bertie looked along the shelves –
there was no way he could read this
many books. He might as well face it –
the quiz was going to be one big
disaster. They would end up losing by a
zillion points and Miss Boot would blame
him as usual. He trawled through the
books gloomily. *Ancient Kings and Queens,*
Fun with Fossils, My First Book of
Flowers… Wait a minute, what was this?

"Gran!" called Bertie. "Can I get this
one out?"

"Of course!"
said Gran.
"What is it?"

Bertie held
up the cover
so she could
read it.

CHAPTER 3

For the next two weeks, the quiz team
met to practise every lunchtime. Things
did not improve. Nick grumbled that he
was leading a team of idiots, even though
Donna and Eugene were quite good.
Sadly the same could not be said of
Bertie. The one time he got an answer
right, he ran round the room yelling with

his T-shirt over his head.

All too soon, the day of the Junior Quiz Challenge arrived. Pudsley had been drawn to face last year's finalists, Swotter House. As the coach pulled into the drive, Bertie stared up at the ancient-looking school. Miss Topping, one of the teachers, was waiting to meet them at the door.

"Miss Boot, welcome!" she beamed. "And this must be your quiz team!"

"Yes," said Miss Boot. "This is Nicholas, Donna, Eugene and ... don't do that please, Bertie."

Bertie removed a finger that had crept up his nose. He wiped it on his jumper to show he hadn't forgotten his manners.

"Well," said Miss Topping brightly,

"I'm sure they're cleverer than they look. May I introduce our team? This is Giles, Miles, Tara and Harriet. They are so looking forward to beating ... I mean meeting you."

The Swotter House team shook hands solemnly. They wore spotless purple blazers and neatly knotted ties. Bertie thought they looked like they all belonged to the same family – the Frankenstein family.

Dirty Bertie

At two o'clock people began to file into the hall for the start of the quiz. The two teams were seated opposite each other on the stage. The Swotter House team sat up straight. The Pudsley team fidgeted nervously. Miss Boot was in the front row next to Miss Skinner. The hall was filling up with supporters from both schools. Bertie wondered if he should make a run for it now. Know-All Nick leaned over to give his team talk.

"Remember," he whispered. "I'm captain, so let me handle the questions."

"Yeah, but what if you don't know the answers?" said Bertie.

Nick rolled his eyes. "Trust me, I know what I'm doing," he said.

Donna and Eugene exchanged worried looks. But it was too late to argue now, Miss Topping was taking her seat and the quiz was about to start. The hall lights dimmed. The audience chatter died down. Miss Topping began by explaining the rules.

"The first team to buzz may answer," she said. "If you get it wrong, the question passes to the other team."

Both teams nodded. The Junior Quiz Challenge began.

"What do the letters MP stand for?" said Miss Topping.

BUZZ!

"More pudding!" shouted Nick.

"No, I'll pass it over," said Miss Topping.

"Member of Parliament," answered Giles.

"Correct! Who invented the telephone?"

BUZZ! Nick was first again.

"Um…" he said, going red. "Er … it was…"

"Time's up," said Miss Topping. "Swotter House?"

"Alexander Graham Bell," answered Giles.

"Correct!"

SWOTTER 18

PUDSLEY 01

CHAPTER 4

The questions went on – and on.
By round three Pudsley were trailing
miserably by 18 points to one. Nick had
answered nineteen questions, and got
eighteen of them wrong.

"What are you doing?" moaned
Donna, when they stopped for a
drinks break.

"We have to buzz first or we'll lose!" said Nick.

"We *are* losing," said Bertie.

"What's the good of buzzing first if you don't know the answer?" complained Eugene.

"It's not my fault!" grumbled Nick. "The questions are too hard!"

"Well, if you carry on like this they're going to batter us," said Bertie.

"Yes, and so will Miss Boot," said Eugene.

They glanced over at their class teacher whose face was like thunder.

"Let me or Eugene answer for a change," said Donna.

"What about me?" asked Bertie.

"Er, well, you too," said Donna. "But only if you're sure you know the answer."

Round four got under way. It was about books.

"Who wrote *The BFG*?"

BUZZ!

Donna got there first.

"Roald Dahl," she answered.

"Correct!"

"Can you name the Famous Five?"

BUZZ!

The scoreboard ticked over. Three rounds later, Swotter House were not looking quite so smug. Thanks to Donna and Eugene, Pudsley had closed the gap to just three points at 34 points to 31. Bertie had still not spoken a word, except to ask if he could go to the toilet. Now everything depended on the final round. The teams leaned forward.

"Our final round is about the human body," said Miss Topping.

Bertie suddenly sat up, paying attention. This was more like it. He'd been reading *Why are Bogeys Green?*, which had a lot to say about the human body.

"What is saliva?" asked Miss Topping.

BUZZ!

"A disease?" asked Giles.

"No, I'm afraid not."

"I know!" shouted Bertie. He buzzed. "Spit!"

"Correct," said Miss Topping. "Which part of the body has half a million sweat glands?"

BUZZ!

"YOUR FEET!" yelled Bertie.

"Correct. What do you produce more of when you're scared?"

BUZZ!

"EARWAX!" cried Bertie.

His teammates stared at him. Surely this had to be wrong?

"Correct!" said Miss Topping. "What—"

BEEP! BEEP! BEEP! The timer interrupted, bringing the quiz to an end. The scores were level at 34 points each. Miss Topping announced the contest would be decided by a tiebreak question.

"Whoever answers correctly is the winner," she said, glaring at the Swotter House team.

The teams sat on the edge of their seats, their fingers poised to buzz. Miss Boot chewed her fingernails.

Dirty Bertie

"What did the Romans use as toothpaste?" asked Miss Topping.

The hall fell deadly silent. Seven faces looked blank. Bertie shut his eyes, trying to remember. Toothpaste, what did the Romans use as toothpaste – hadn't he read this somewhere? It was something to do with squirrels or hamsters or…

BUZZ!

"Was it yoghurt?" asked Harriet.

"No. Pudsley, can you answer?"

Everyone turned to Bertie. He opened his eyes.

"MOUSE BRAINS!" he cried.

"EWWW!" groaned the audience. Miss Boot sunk her head in her hands. Trust Bertie to ruin everything.

Dirty Bertie

Miss Topping sighed deeply. "Correct," she said. "Pudsley are the winners."

A deafening cheer shook the hall. Know-All Nick was speechless. Miss Boot and Miss Skinner hugged and danced round the room. For the first time ever, Pudsley had won a quiz contest, and Bertie, of all people, had answered the winning question. He ran round the stage yelling, until he was carried off by his cheering teammates.

"Well, we did it," said Eugene, as they finally left the hall.

"Yes," said Bertie. "Thank goodness it's all over."

"Until next time," said Miss Boot.

Bertie stared at her. "N-next time?"

"Of course," said Miss Boot. "That was just the first round. There's six more before you reach the final!" She thumped him hard on the back. "And we are all counting on you, Bertie!"